Sacrament and Smoke
A Blood and Rubies Short Story

Kathryn Trattner

Copyright © 2024 by Kathryn Trattner

Magic and Myth Media LLC

All rights reserved.

No part of this book may be reproduced in any form or by any electronic or mechanical means, including information storage and retrieval systems, without written permission from the author, except for the use of brief quotations in a book review.

eBook ISBN: 979-8-9872112-7-4

Paperback ISBN: 978-1-962327-03-9

Editor: Indie Edits with Jeanine

Cover Designer: Jineus Covers

www.kathryntrattner.com

Please be aware this story includes: death, a tiny bit of cannibalism, suicide, and other dark themes.

In all of time,
I wonder how
many lives I
will have to
live, until I
find my way
back to you.

- d.j.

THE WORLD OF BLOOD AND RUBIES
WINTER PALACE
SUMMER PALACE
GREEN TEMPLE
MARE TESTA
RED TOWER

Contents

Chapter 1	1
Chapter 2	13
Chapter 3	20
Chapter 4	22
Chapter 5	33
Chapter 6	39
What Came After	48
Keep reading for a sneak peek at The Dead Saint	51
The Dead Saint - Chapter One	52
The Dead Saint - Chapter Two	60
About the Author	67
Also by Kathryn Trattner	69

Chapter One

In the night sky, a golden star burst into life—birthed from the promise of sorrow and pain—glittering on the horizon.

The end and the beginning of all things.

Midnight came and went, and yet the banquet hall remained crowded. People clung to merriment with both hands, drinking wine and eating sweets as they watched each other, waiting for someone else to leave first. No one wanted to miss what might happen with the strangers—*creatures*—moving among them.

Kira sat in a bubble of calm—the party circling without ever including her. No one wanted to draw the attention of the oracle. The thought that she could touch them and know the time and place of their death terrified them. It wasn't that simple, but it didn't matter. They avoided her anyway.

She adjusted the gold bangles on her wrist and sipped

sweet wine, watching the room. The bottom of the glass was full of fruit—oranges, cherries, and other varieties she'd never seen before. All had been presented to the Saint as gifts. Kira glanced around, searching for her friend to return to their seats with the promised food. She'd been gone for close to twenty minutes now. Something—or *someone*—must have distracted August.

Monsters and men filled the hall. Emissaries from neighboring kingdoms arrived at the temple first, ignoring protocol to present themselves in court to King Caspian before seeing Hakan. They'd traveled from cities over the mountains to the west and sea islands to the east, wearing the fashions of their cultures, their words thick with accents Kira had never encountered before.

Delegates waited to hear Hakan's plans for unification, prepared to take his offer back or answer as they'd been previously instructed. Some would say yes, others no. Not everyone would follow a self-proclaimed saint. Many would rather lead their own lives than fall under the rule or guidance of another. Or follow the spoiled inclinations of young King Caspian. The entire continent watched and waited as the kingdoms to the south broke apart into smaller and smaller factions.

War was coming, and Hakan believed he could stop it.

Kira glanced around the hall. Was he with one of the lords? Or had one of the creatures caught his attention? She'd hoped to see him before the event began, but he'd been behind guarded doors since dawn. And she'd been in the inner temple, focusing on the quiet of her mind and desperately searching the future.

Kahina Alexandra had pressed her hard for clear images—anything solid they could take to the council. There had been fire and rubies, a flash of gold, a blade burning in a dark place. Nothing made sense—it hadn't for months. So, each day, she secluded herself and searched, desperate to find the one piece that would link these images together.

Tomorrow, she would join Kahina Alexandra in the inner sanctum and try again. King Caspian demanded answers while Hakan quietly requested them. Either way, she needed to decipher the visions. A feeling—nothing as solid as fear or dread—had grown like a creeping vine through her mind over the last year. Alexandra insisted that everything was fine. August dismissed Kira's worries. And Hakan? He changed the subject every time she brought it up.

Finally, she saw him at a far table, surrounded by creatures, nodding thoughtfully as a tall, thin being wrapped in a black cloak and hood gestured with an elegant hand. Kira shivered as she watched them. Myths and legends filled the hall tonight—dreams and nightmares crowded around her.

Tonight was a turning point for them all as the city watched the magic in the world materialize and walk through the temple doors. These creatures had come when Hakan called, answering his invitation or demand. To some, this power confirmed his sainthood. To others, it was another sign he'd grown too powerful. The creatures unnerved those who ruled the surrounding lands. What power could a king or emperor hold on to if, at any moment, vampires and werewolves, stone guardians of the lakes and streams, or the other myriad of living myths could overrun them?

Kira sipped her wine and swirled the remainder in the glass—alcohol-soaked fruit sloshing back and forth. The surrounding conversations were loud, full of boasts and bets, promises being made that might never be kept. She smiled, hoping that at least a few of them might come true. Maybe tomorrow she would see which ones those might be.

"Enjoying yourself, Kira?"

The voice caught her off guard, and she straightened,

looking up into Kahina Alexandra's face. Kira's mentor looked the same as she had the day they'd met. Darkly beautiful—like a polished river stone or piece of navy-blue velvet. Pale brown eyes searched her face, and Kira wondered what the woman was hoping to find.

"Yes, Kahina."

"Please." Kahina Alexandra waved one jewel-encrusted hand. "No titles tonight. I'm Alexandra here."

Kira nodded but couldn't bring herself not to use the title. It was a matter of respect. And though their relationship had grown over the years, Alexandra would always be a parental figure. She was also the second most senior figure in the temple. Only Hakan held a higher position of honor.

"What do you think?" Alexandra lifted her chin in the direction of Hakan. "Of these creatures he's called out of the wild?"

"I think they could make powerful allies," Kira said, choosing her words carefully.

There was an edge to her mentor's question. She glanced at the woman and then away, putting on a pleasant half smile and smoothing the line of worry that had formed between her brows.

"Do you?" Alexandra chuckled. "Well, maybe you're right."

I am right, Kira thought. *I might not have deciphered the repeated images in my visions, but I know in my bones that these creatures here tonight will remain loyal to Hakan no matter what happens.* A treacherous thought followed. *Then who here will betray him?*

"What time tomorrow would you like me to meet you?" Kira asked, glancing around for August. For the first time she could remember, she wanted to end a conversation with Alexandra. Something about the woman felt different tonight—dangerous. "I can be there after the morning call to prayer."

Sooner even, Kira thought. Hakan's rooms were closer to the sanctuary than Kira's quarters.

"Tomorrow?" Alexandra scanned the room, her gaze lingering on a group of priests and priestesses talking among themselves. She brushed her black hair away from her face—rings flashing, bracelets tinkling a brief song.

"Yes, I—" Kira began.

"Don't worry about tomorrow," Alexandra cut in. "Here comes your friend. August is her name?"

Kira nodded.

"Keep her close tonight," Alexandra said, stepping away. "We'll see each other soon."

Before Kira could say anything else, her mentor melted back into the crowd.

Soon. What did Alexandra mean by that? Soon, but not in the morning?

Kira looked around, spotting August making her way over to their table, but the older woman was gone.

"What did the kahina want?" August asked, sliding a plate piled high with cakes toward Kira and setting a pitcher of wine down with a thump. She sighed as she took up her place, sliding the plate to sit between them, and gulped half her wine. "Are you needed somewhere else?"

"No." Kira shook her head. Her gaze returned to Hakan, and she bit her lip, considering Alexandra's odd response. "She wanted to know if I was enjoying the party. And how I felt about the guests."

August waggled her eyebrows, a smile growing as she leaned closer to Kira. "Do you think it's true about the blood drinkers? Some say their bite is as pleasurable as sex."

"What?" Kira asked, her gaze leaving Hakan and traveling in search of the creatures August was curious about.

A small contingent was gathered in the center of the room. The nightwalkers were all striking, with pale skin and reflective eyes, sharp teeth visible as they laughed. Would their bite be as sweet as the moment before Hakan slid inside her? It was hard to imagine it could be true.

"I heard someone say they can't walk in the day." August popped a bite of cake in her mouth, chewing thoughtfully. "But they arrived here in the daylight, so I suppose that part isn't true. Do you think the sex part is?"

"You could always ask," Kira suggested with a smile.

"No." August shook her head. She wasn't the type of woman to ask too many questions of those people she didn't count as close friends. Being at the bottom of the temple hierarchy meant doing what you were told. Not asking questions or fishing for answers. "But you could. You've been officially introduced."

"Not really." Kira sipped her wine, ignoring the cloying taste and concentrating on the way the glass felt in her hand. Solid yet breakable, a parallel to how she felt right at this moment. "I merely stood in the line to greet everyone as they entered. I don't even know how I would start that conversation."

"One of them kissed your hand. I think I actually gasped aloud. And he's so handsome." August gave her a wicked smile. "Were his lips cold?"

"No," Kira said, remembering the dark-haired man with the strange reflective eyes.

His lips had been warm on her skin, his touch light. The woman beside him was equally beautiful, with fine-boned features and auburn hair. She'd given Kira a nod but nothing else.

They'd been the only ones to touch her. Blood drinkers. Vampires. Nightwalkers. Even fabled creatures were afraid the oracle would see something bleak in their future. But Kira saw nothing—felt nothing—but the confidence in his touch.

"And the others?" August pressed, watching Kira with curiosity.

"Like we are, I suppose," Kira said, shrugging. "Like people."

There were shifters and witches, demons and fallen angels, strange beings with light beneath their skin and blood mages with red eyes, men made of stone, and other beings that were merely shadows. Hakan warned Kira about what to expect the night before, so she'd been one of the few prepared for such a strange meeting.

The murmuring in the reception hall had risen, voice after voice climbing above the other in wonder or fear. Most were curious in a benign way, like August. Her friend had whispered in her ear, pointing or indicating some strange new being. They'd each wondered what it might be like to know this person or that.

There were those in the room who did not share August's curiosity. Kira watched them carefully, gaze never lingering too long, not wanting to draw their attention. The older priests and priestesses wore grim expressions in their fine crimson robes—adorned with golden brooches and faceted stones—delicate rings, and heavy bracelets shifting and making dull music as they moved.

Zavier was there, Kahina Alexandra's confidant, and Kira would have expected her mentor to be beside him. But the woman was gone. Kira turned, scanning the space, an uneasiness creeping in.

"What are they thinking?" Kira asked, nodding toward the older group.

"Well." August shrugged. "I'm sure they're not happy. They're so old fashioned, but they trust him. They know he'll do what's best for us."

"Do they?" Kira asked, voice sharp.

"Of course!" August patted Kira's hand. "Please, don't do this tonight. I know you've been worried, but tonight is about enjoying the moment."

Kira nodded, but she continued to watch the group as inconspicuously as possible. They were set apart from the others, putting on a show for those who watched—those who might question their loyalty to Hakan. They wore their temple wealth like armor, a barrier between themselves and those they considered unworthy—protection from the creatures with no right to be here.

Tomorrow, there would be angry shouts and accusations about being left out of Hakan's plans—raised voices would ring throughout the corridors. He hadn't consulted the temple elders before he'd extended his invitation to emissaries and monsters. They would present a united front now, but it would be different in the morning.

"He's staring at you," August whispered. "I swear, he could set the world on fire with those eyes."

Kira smiled, turning to meet Hakan's gaze across the room. Warmth suffused her body. His blue eyes hinted at a smile, even as he kept his expression thoughtful for the person speaking intently beside him. A blush fanned across her cheeks, stomach fluttering at the thought of moments they'd shared last night—his lips hot on her neck, tracing the curve of her shoulder, teeth scraping against tender skin.

Covering her mouth, she worked to hide the wide smile, and Hakan looked away. But she knew he felt the pull of her desire. Each time their eyes met—across a crowded room, during temple meetings, in the half-light of his rooms in the evening—it was there between them.

Kira studied him, surrounded as he was by a room full of people and creatures. A tall man with broad shoulders, long blond hair, and blue eyes that shifted to gray, reflecting the sky and whatever emotions he picked up from those around him.

For her, his eyes were always that deep blue of clear ocean water, pupils dilated and dark. This evening, he practically glowed, a beacon drawing all eyes toward him.

And yet, her gaze was the one Hakan searched out.

"Will you go to him tonight?" August asked, leaning in to whisper, though there was no one near to overhear. She grinned, raising her eyebrows. "Do you want me to wait for you?"

"You don't have to wait," Kira said, glancing at her friend with a smile.

"I don't know why I offered." August laughed. "Of course you'll be there until dawn. You'll have to meet me in the baths in the morning, and we can exchange stories about our night."

"What will you do?" Kira asked.

They'd never actually shared the most private details of their nights. Or at least they'd stopped when Kira found herself in Hakan's bed—one night had turned into weeks and then months. It didn't feel appropriate to share the details of the Saint's personal life.

"I'm not opposed to getting to know some of the visitors better." August's grin widened. Her brown eyes swept the room, searching for the perfect target. Several men looked like her type—tall and handsome, with roguish grins and lots of muscles. But her gaze kept coming back to the blood drinkers. "Who knows how the night will end?"

"Please be careful," Kira said, reaching out to squeeze August's arm. "Don't go too far tonight."

"I told you"—August patted Kira's hand—"you worry too much. Nothing is going to happen."

Kira opened her mouth, but August held up a hand.

The visions had been so disjointed and shadowed, a string of images held together with little meaning. Even Kahina Alexandra had struggled to decipher them. The two had spent hours together in the inner temple, sitting in complete silence to contemplate the intricacies.

"I'm not discounting your visions. I know they worry you. But with so many people here, all these politicians and royals and creatures, no one would dare make any kind of move against Hakan." August waved a hand languidly. "There are too many important people in one place."

"Maybe that makes it the perfect time," Kira said softly, leaning toward her friend to make sure no one overheard them.

"The king is a believer," August said with a shrug. "As was his father. No one will go against him."

"But there are many in the court who are not. And August." Kira motioned for her friend to come closer as she lowered her voice further. "There are emissaries here who didn't stop to pay their respects to the king first. They came straight to the temple. What king would tolerate such a thing?"

"It doesn't matter." August shook her head, glancing around the room. "As long as King Caspian supports us, no one will defy him. You shouldn't let worry steal your peace. This is an evening to enjoy. A celebration!"

Kira smiled but a hint of worry remained.

"August—" She began, then stopped, gaze shifting over the room. She let out a breath and smiled. "You're right. Nothing will happen. I'm being overly cautious."

"You always are," August said, gulping down more wine and grimacing. "I need something else. This is terrible stuff. Would you like something?"

Kira shook her head. "No, thank you."

"Don't leave without letting me know. Otherwise, I'll worry that one of these shifters carried you off into the night," August said with a hint of teasing. "Or invite me along, at least."

"Nothing like that will happen," Kira said with a laugh.

"Of course not. Because we all know whose bed you'll be in." August smiled, leaning over the back of her chair toward Kira—half laughing, half serious. "On second thought, if you're not here when I get back, I won't worry at all because you'll already be naked beneath Hakan."

"Shush!" Kira said, waving at her friend to leave.

August made her way around the banquet tables, pausing to talk to a group of lower priests, skirting groups of creatures.

A tall, dark man with glowing yellow eyes turned to watch her pass, intense curiosity on his handsome face. Kira laughed when August smiled at him, an obvious invitation in her expression. According to August, if you were handsome, you weren't a threat. Hopefully, she'd enjoy her time with this stranger.

Her gaze drifted back to Hakan, excitement building in her chest when he stood and gave the table a few last words. It was hard to read their faces, but Kira supposed they looked pleased. Maybe they'd brokered a new treaty or negotiated for some concession with the temple. These days, the temple's reach was far and wide. Hakan had expanded it well beyond the walls of the Golden Citadel. He'd turned religion into an army and claimed all who answered his call as his soldiers.

She'd foreseen his success. In her vision, he'd been at a great distance, leading an army, a golden figure on a barren plain, wearing strange armor glittering in the rays of a dying sun. He'd risen head and shoulders above those around him—as Hakan did now—and seemed to pull all available light toward him, reflecting it outward.

Kira smiled when she caught his gaze again, thrilled with the small nod he gave her. A signal that anyone would have seen if they'd been paying attention. And surely, someone must have. But most of the people within the temple didn't care. It was the others, the people who lived beyond these walls, that expected an inhuman perfection from their Saint.

Glancing around, Kira searched for August, but her friend was nowhere to be seen. Neither was the man with the striking yellow eyes. Kira smiled, hoping the two were enjoying themselves.

Chapter Two

Beyond the smoky hall, with the sounds of conversation and laughter fading, the air was cool and clear. Kira took a deep breath, enjoying the quiet, as she made her way down the corridor. Pillars rose on either side, disappearing into the painted ceiling high overhead. Only a handful of braziers were lit, spaced far apart, shadows gathering between them as the night slunk in to explore the festivities.

To the left, the space between the pillars was open, leading out into an inner courtyard filled with night-blooming flowers —their scent reached her as a breeze rustled the tall, narrow trees. Kira caught glimpses of the stars as she walked—dress swishing around her ankles—anticipation building at the thought of Hakan and the wicked curve of his lips.

Kira yelped as a figure lunged out of the shadows between two pillars. He picked her up and swung her around in a tight circle, and a low, rumbling chuckle vibrated through her. The scent of warm amber and deep water washed over her, filling her senses, recalling a thousand tiny, shared moments. *Hakan.* His touch was everything she'd craved. It had been torture to be so close to him and not be able to reach out and feel his warmth.

"You scared me!" Kira laughed, settling her hands on his shoulders, enjoying the strength in them.

Her hair slipped out of the loose knot at the back of her neck, rippling down and falling around his face. He grinned, a dimple flashing, laughter filling his eyes.

Hakan. The golden Saint. A man who was more than a man.

"You can't tell me you didn't know it was me," he said and lowered her slowly down his body, her breasts pushed flat to his chest.

He dipped his head, mouth hovering over her own, a slight smile curving at the corners, waiting for her.

Kira pushed up on her toes, kissing him, pulling him down to her. His arms went around her again, lifting her once more—this time gently, slowly, as they clung to each other. He tasted of spiced wine and a hint of roasted apples. Sweet and heady.

She made a small noise of pleasure, and his arms tightened.

She broke the kiss as he set her down once more, her hands pressed flat against the hard muscles of his chest. The tunic he wore was simple cotton—a blue so dark it was almost black. Between one breath and the next, Kira searched his face earnestly, looking for something she had no name for.

"Why so jumpy?" he asked, pressing a kiss to her jaw, another to the tender spot beneath her ear. His hands were in her hair, tilting her face to expose more of her neck and the line of her collarbones.

Her gaze drifted down the long hall to where the party continued beyond half-open wall hangings. That room, full of political maneuverings and creatures, didn't exactly worry her, but it came close. Too many muddled visions—armies and golden stars, a blade made of burning bone. She curled her fingers into Hakan's tunic.

"Kira," he murmured, leaning back and studying her face. "No one will ever hurt you here."

"I've seen . . . things." Kira began, lowering her voice, her hand touching his temple. His blue eyes became somber, a line appearing between his brows. She traced the wrinkle, smoothing it out. "Kahina Alexandra hasn't been able to decipher the meaning. There have been so many whispered conversations. And I know the elders are angry you didn't warn them about tonight."

She'd wanted to embrace August's carefree attitude, but her fears were rooted deep—growing in the back of her mind and difficult to ignore. Kira trusted August, and if she wasn't worried, why was it eating away at her?

Hakan's expression gave her nothing. He wore that flat calm he employed in the temple meetings and at court.

If he was worried—in any way, no matter how small—he wasn't sharing with her.

"There are always whispers, Kira."

"But these—"

"You have nothing to worry about," Hakan said, pressing a kiss to her temple and pulling her into him. "Come to bed with me. Let's forget everyone else for a little while."

Kira nodded, sucking in a deep breath and banishing the doubt.

"Your Reverence, do you have a moment?" Zavier coughed discreetly, his eyes shifting from Kira's face to Hakan's hands on her waist. "In private?"

"Of course," Hakan said, glancing away from Kira, his hands remaining at her waist. His voice changed when he spoke to the others—deeper, more somber. With them, he was the god wrapped in flesh and bone, alive but immortal and all-knowing. "Let's go to the sanctuary. It's quieter there."

Kira stepped back as he moved around her, his fingers lingering a moment. Their eyes met briefly—a question and an answer passing between them. She would see him later, in the privacy of his room. She wondered briefly how long she would have to wait. Zavier had worn a serious expression.

The light and noise of the banquet cut through Kira's thoughts. Hakan could be hours. Serious discussions could take all night. Kira went back toward the light, leaving the shadows of the outer temple, unaware of the figure watching from the gloom.

"You came," Hakan said, a smile hovering around his generous mouth—light flashing in his blue eyes.

He held his arms wide, welcoming her, calling her home.

Kira went to him—compelled—unable to resist his draw. The curl of his deep voice in her ear promised delicious things.

"I'll always come," she said, stepping into the circle of his arms.

"I was almost positive you'd decided to stay to drink with August."

"No." Kira rubbed her cheek against his chest. "She found someone else to drink with. I'm sure she's having a delightful time."

Hakan laughed, holding her close, and pressed a kiss into her hair.

She'd been unable to banish the unease stalking her all evening. August had been dismissive, not cruel but uninterested and more concerned with the man with the yellow eyes. Kira had had two more glasses of wine and watched the crowd without seeing them, considering their future. Everything was changing, and right now, she needed reassurance—she needed to know they'd come out the other side of these trials whole and safe.

"Have you heard about the separatists?" she asked.

She waited for him to respond—to fill the growing silence—as her thoughts drifted to the past, even as she contemplated the future. Kira came to the temple as an adult. Her gift had shown itself later in life, and the priests in her village considered her too old to train. But Alexandra had come from the Golden Citadel to meet this new oracle and test her strengths. Kira's path had been set the moment their hands touched—power recognizing power.

They'd departed for the Citadel that very hour, leaving behind everything Kira had ever known. She'd found the rhythm in her life easily, slipping into the complicated structure of priests and priestesses. In the temple, her talents were fostered and grew, and Kira's visions of the future were shared with those who might understand them better than herself.

It had always been that way for Kira—she saw images and felt things, but none of it made much sense to her. They came as a fog of pictures and emotion, leaving her muddled and blinking like a newborn in their aftermath.

But in the past year, unrest had grown, fostered by those who felt it a mistake to pin all their hopes and dreams on a single god. The temples of the Citadel had been dedicated to older gods and goddesses—Delphine, Tetum, and the Seven. But it was Hakan the people prayed to now. The emissaries turned to him, and it was the king who bent his head to listen. The separatists wanted a return to the world before Hakan had appeared and claimed to be the only one capable of answering their prayers.

"I know about them," he said finally, voice low.

Hakan rested his chin on the top of her head, smoothing his large hands over her shoulder blades and down her back. Whatever he might have heard, or might feel, he wouldn't tell her. No matter how Kira pressed the issue, his thoughts remained private. Even as the disquiet grew, even as warning bells rang, he refused to let her in.

"What will you do?" she whispered.

"What they expect me to do," Hakan said.

"And what is that?"

"Kira." He tilted back, looking down at her, moving her a little away from his body so she would have to meet his gaze. "This will get us nowhere. There's no point in talking about these things."

"It would make me feel better."

"No," he said, shaking his head. "It will only add to your worries. Leave that to me. Your shoulders weren't meant to carry such a burden."

Not meant to carry such a burden. But always welcome in his bed.

The thought surprised her, a sign of how worried Kira had become no matter how much she denied it. A golden star had appeared on the horizon a few days ago. A harbinger of impending destruction. But whose destruction, Kahina Alexandra could not say.

Ours.

It was an insidious thought.

Kira squeezed her eyes shut, cutting off the warm light thrown by the braziers dotted around the high-ceilinged room and the candles beside the bed on the dais. The room was a shimmering sea of crimson and gold—his colors.

The colors of a Saint.

"Let me ease your mind, Kira," Hakan said, voice roughening.

He moved to cup her breasts, hands moving deliberately, knowing her body as well as he knew his own. He pulled a shivering gasp from her throat as she tangled her hands in his hair. When he kissed her, Kira met him, hungry for the forgetfulness he offered. Her simple dress was over her head in an instant, and he knelt before her, pressing kisses to delicate flesh while gripping her hips tightly. Her eyes fluttered closed, welcoming the pleasure and impending release—grateful for the way it washed her mind clean of all other things.

Chapter Three

Afterward, in silence, Hakan wove his fingers through her hair—tender and slow. Here, in the privacy of his rooms, his touch was so different from that of the man who sat in the temple to dispense justice.

"I love you," she whispered for the thousandth time—for the hundred thousandth.

It ached, the emotion hot in her chest—to love and be loved by a being of eternity and yet still feel so uncertain about the future.

"In every lifetime," he murmured.

Hakan pulled Kira toward him and kissed her. His hands were everywhere, and a tingling warmth gathered low in her belly. Her skin was alive beneath his touch. Without him, the world was a dull, gray place. Only Hakan brought vibrancy.

But the worry had returned, insistent and inescapable.

"Please," Kira said, propping herself up on an elbow to look down at him—her golden Saint, a god in the shape of a man. "Tell me how this ends. You know, you've seen it all. I've heard what the high priestess has said. I know what the elders think."

Hakan studied her face, a line forming between his brows. She reached out, running her fingertips lightly over his face, cupping his warm cheek.

"Death is not the end, Kira." He took her face in his hands. "Remember that."

She shook her head, a protest on her tongue, frustration constricting her throat.

"Come back to me," Hakan said, pulling her down to his chest and making soothing sounds. He traced the line of her shoulder, her spine, murmuring against her hair. "Sleep."

Kira listened to the steady beat of his heart—one that sounded so like her own and yet slightly different. A double beat, a stutter, a fluttering in his chest so unlike any other she'd lain awake listening to. There was something otherworldly about him in the quiet moments they shared.

She'd seen the miracles firsthand—people brought back from death, barren fields suddenly fruitful. She'd seen the creatures arriving laden with gifts. Witnessed nobility from distant lands bring tribute and ask for blessings.

Kira could not forget that Hakan was not a man.

Chapter Four

"Kira."

A hand was on her shoulder, insistent pressure demanding her attention. It dragged her up from dark dreams—a vast grassy plain where two armies clashed. The vision clung to Kira, catching in the cracks of her mind, wrapped in an uneasy sense of certainty. It left her with a pounding heart and a terrible cold spot in the center of her chest.

"Wake up."

Kira opened her eyes, blinking rapidly.

August stood over her, face shadowed. "It's happened," she whispered. "They've come."

"What?"

Kira sat up, fully awake now. In the dim light thrown by a single flickering brazier, she could barely see August—tall and straight with her heart-shaped face and lovely dark eyes. A few hours ago, she'd smiled and laughed, and toasted the coming dawn. She'd brushed off Kira's worry. Now, she stood here grimly, surrounded by a tangle of emotions and heavy with the scent of fear.

"We need to leave," August said, grabbing the dress crumpled at the foot of the bed. She tossed the garment at Kira, a flapping creature made of crimson silk, which landed in Kira's lap with a whisper. "Get dressed."

Kira looked around the room. Hakan was gone. All the braziers except for one had died down, and an early morning chill filled the space. She'd fallen asleep. Finally soothed by his touch. The room had been bright and warm then as they lay there tangled in crimson sheets. She reached out, running a hand across the spot he'd occupied in the bed. It was cold. He'd been gone for some time.

"Where is he?"

"Soldiers are moving through the city. I think there are assassins in the temple. The shadows are *moving*, Kira."

"Where—"

"I don't know. He wasn't here when I came in."

Kira stared straight ahead, mind racing.

"Please, we have to go." August spoke sharply, turning to look at the door, twisting her hands together. "You have to get dressed."

"But he was here." Kira gestured at the bed, the room with its walls covered in murals and the floor covered in woven carpets. The gilded ceiling overhead moved with shadows as the last brazier flickered, the light fading—dying second by second. "I have to find him!"

"Come with me now," August pleaded. "He'll be fine."

The note of panic in August's voice finally caught Kira's attention. The calm demeanor she'd been able to cultivate at first was gone—only terror remained. Kira slipped out of the bed and pulled the dress up, fastening the simple clasps at her shoulders. Her fingers shook slightly, tension coiling in her body, settling in her jaw and neck. She moved to light the other braziers, wanting the relief they would bring. August stopped her.

"No more light," she said. "They'll see it and come."

"If they're already here, what does it matter?"

But August only shook her head, a hard gleam in her eye as she spoke. "We must go now! *Right now, Kira*. We must. You were right. I was so wrong."

"No," Kira said stubbornly, lifting her chin and pulling her shoulders back.

"Kira." August took a step toward her, hands out, pleading. "You have no other choice."

"I do." Kira made a sharp motion with her hand, dismissing August's words. "You go if you want."

"If you don't leave now, you might not make it out."

"They won't do anything to me." But even as Kira said it, she wasn't sure. She repeated the words, willing them to be true, to reflect the future before her. "They *won't* hurt me."

"You don't know that," August said, voice soft, a whine weaving through the words. "You don't understand the things you've seen."

"I'm the oracle," Kira laughed. A bitter edge sharpened her words, and beneath the bravado came a hint of doubt. "They need me to see their futures. They won't hurt me."

They need me to see their deaths.

"You think so?" August's voice was cutting, lashing out with anger or fear. Kira wasn't sure which. "The woman who tempted a saint? The woman who infected him and took away his purity? He's no longer the creature they wanted him to be. Alexandra warned you."

"When has that ever mattered before?" Kira raised her hands, genuine confusion filling her.

Hakan had had other lovers, held other women, and been loved. But when the oracle came to his bed, it was different.

"Because you're the oracle."

"But it's only a small fraction of the community that's upset. These are zealots. Extremists. The rest of us do not believe as they do. Even Kahina Alexandra doesn't believe."

Kira lifted her hands with a shrug. "She's only suggested more discretion."

"It doesn't matter," August wailed, throwing her hands in the air and taking a step back—turning to pace like a cornered animal. "They might be the minority, but they are dangerous. They are *here*. And you will not survive if you stay."

Kira shook her head, denying the fear threatening to overwhelm them both.

"You must come with me." August turned back to her, coming forward with her hands out. "I love you, you're my dearest friend. This will blow over in time. They will have gotten what they wanted. Eventually, they'll forget about you."

"I won't leave Hakan," Kira whispered, emotion welling up, tears gathering in her eyes with August's words.

Would they? Or would they carry their grudge with them? This might be the only chance Kira had to stand her ground. If she ran, she would have to keep running, and they would chase her.

"You'll die," August said flatly. Defeat made her sag, pulling at the corners of her mouth and dragging down her shoulders.

Kira swallowed, stomach fluttering. When she spoke, her voice was hard. "It's not worth living without him."

"You're a fool," August said. "And I won't stay to watch you die."

"Death is not the end," she whispered, remembering Hakan's words.

"What?" August's voice rose sharply. "Are you welcoming death, then?"

"Go. If you're afraid of them, then go. But I refuse to run. Even in their self-righteousness, they won't do anything. They're cowards. And he is still the Saint."

"He's tainted, Kira." August swallowed. "He's fallen."

"They still believe. Nothing will happen as long as they still believe."

"Kira," August whispered, hands out in a pleading gesture.

"Do you believe?" Kira asked, everything inside her taut, knotting together.

She watched her friend with growing desperation. This was a woman who had become dearer to Kira than any sister. If August had abandoned all faith . . . the thought was more than she could bear.

"Of course I do," August replied, anguish radiating outward. "I've seen the miracles. I've experienced them. But there are people out there—priests and priestesses even—who have never seen Hakan. They claim to have faith but fail to believe. These are the people who are here now, people who have never truly believed but used Hakan's name to draw power to themselves."

Tears slipped down August's cheeks. She swiped at them, mouth trembling. In the dim light, the tears reflected the dying fire, ribbons of molten emotion tracking down her face.

"What about the others? The creatures? Emissaries?"

"Scattered. There were only a few left in the banquet hall, and the others had retired to their beds or melted into the city. I've only seen temple members since I came to wake you."

Kira nodded as she took August's hands, pulling her into a tight embrace. *Please don't let this be the last time I see you*, she thought.

"I will see you soon," Kira whispered, releasing her friend and stepping back.

"I hope so." August nodded, giving Kira a trembling smile before fleeing the room—bare feet virtually silent as she escaped.

But her departure barely registered to Kira.

Where was Hakan now? Had an advisor woken him? Was

he alive? Was he safe?

Why did he leave me here?

The question circled beneath the others, darker and deeper down. She tried to ignore it. But it lingered, transforming into fear, driving her forward. The doubt was insidious, blooming beneath her skin, coming to life along her nerves.

A scream—filled with pain and terror—tore through the early morning. It rose, continuing until Kira couldn't stand it any longer and covered her ears. Not August. Someone else. Someone she knew? She couldn't be sure.

With a shudder, she straightened her shoulders and left the Saint's rooms for the last time.

The temple was a riot of confusion.

Kira turned left out of Hakan's rooms, moving toward the common areas of the temple. She followed the sounds of people—shouting, crying, screaming, pleading, threatening. Incense filled the air. The perfume heavy and cloying. Kira choked on every breath she took. The smoke was thick in the back of her throat.

Someone had readied the temple for the new day. Candles were around the room and on the altar—a million tiny flames dancing, the light shivering along the walls and ceiling. Someone had assumed this day would be like any other, a continuation of their lives. Kira covered her mouth, containing the wail threatening to break free of her throat.

With August, it had been easy to be brave, in those quiet rooms with the lingering memory of Hakan. Now, in this new reality, fear gathered at her back, threatening to engulf her.

Men and women ran past, soldiers with splashes of blood on their armor, unsheathed swords in their hands, dark shapes moving in the shadows. Priests in their red tunics carried weapons she'd never seen before, faces grim, and when they met an enemy, there was a clash of steel. She stopped a priest at random, his dark features strained.

"Have you seen him?" she pleaded, gripping his robes tightly, the dull red of the lower temple—a priest who dealt more with the worshippers, the pilgrims, and the intensely devout.

She could see he didn't recognize her, or if he did, he was too full of panic to see the oracle standing before him.

"Move," he said, pushing her roughly out of his way.

Kira stumbled, tripping over the hem of her gown, and fell, striking her head on a pillar. Pain exploded behind her eyes—bright white heat blooming, throbbing. She touched her temple, feeling the broken skin and slick wetness of blood. Transfixed by the redness on her fingertips, she remained sitting while people ran past.

"Get up, Oracle."

Kira looked up into a stranger's face—at a man she'd not seen before dressed in a gray tunic and breaches. There was blood on his black boots. He reached for her, jerking her to her feet, and led her between two pillars and out of the flow of people. He tilted her head, taking in the wound, mouth flattening for an instant.

"You'll be fine. Don't sit in the middle of the floor to be run over."

She nodded, reaching up to touch her head again.

"No," he said, stopping her. "Don't touch it."

"Where is Hakan?" she mumbled, wondering if this man was friend or foe, savior or executioner. "Who are you?"

"Go." He jerked his chin in the direction she'd come. "Find a quiet place. This will be over soon."

"What will?"

"The Saint's death."

"Who are you?" Kira asked again, tone sharper—cutting like a knife.

"Retribution."

He turned, leaving her there, standing in the shadows as people continued to rush past. A group hurried by carrying torches. Oily smoke billowed around the flames, lurking in the hall and rising to obscure the ceiling. The scent stuck in her nose—burned cotton and pitch, a lingering trace of pine. It left the taste of treason on her tongue. The men were chanting, marching together, their determination a wall of noise.

"Kill the false saint!"

―――

"Kira!"

A man's voice. Not one she recognized.

She darted from the doors of the inner temple into the courtyard filled with benches, open to the lightening sky overhead. Dawn was here, the darkness receding in that slow way it does—when the light of day cannot come soon enough, but the night isn't ready to let go.

If this had been any other day, these benches would have been full, the faithful waiting for their Saint to appear in the light of a new day. They would be ready to witness miracles, to be blessed and affirmed. Hakan would be there to comfort and convince.

But now the space was empty, the sounds of fighting coming from all sides, and the rush of someone running after her. A man came out of the shadows to her left, his face obscured by black cloth—only his pale eyes were visible. She screamed and twisted away, but another man was there, blocking her path. He held a sword in one hand and had a bow slung across his back. His face wasn't covered. His expression was hard and merciless, unforgiving.

"Stop," he said, voice ringing out through the courtyard, rattling inside her head.

She froze—a doe pinned beneath a hunter's gaze.

"We don't want her," said a familiar voice.

Kira turned around, surprised to recognize the woman who stepped forward. Alexandra, High Priestess of the Saint, wore the bright crimson of the inner temple—the same color Kira put on every morning.

"Kahina Alexandra," Kira whispered, shaking her head. "Please, you have to help me. I have to find him."

"Leave us," Alexandra said, waving the two men away.

They disappeared into the early morning gloom, melting into the shadows clinging to the edges of the courtyard. But Kira could feel them watching her.

"What are you doing?" Kira asked, resisting the urge to hurl accusations and fighting to keep her voice calm.

Kahina Alexandra was a priestess of the inner circle, a woman who knew each sacred rite and secret text, where the Saint had come from and how the belief and magic fed him and kept him alive. Only a few knew how truly ancient he was and the facts of his life. Alexandra was a woman Kira would have sworn would be faithful and steadfast.

"It's time for a change, Kira."

Kira shook her head, glaring at the older woman now. "There will be a reckoning. No one will stand with traitors."

Alexandra gestured to the main temple doors at the far end. The entire city lay beneath this place of worship, gathered around like children at the feet of a revered teacher.

"Come see," Alexandra invited—face serene but the glint of something vicious in her gaze.

Kira followed the woman—once a mentor and friend—warily, keeping her distance. As Alexandra pushed open the doors, Kira gasped. The terrace was full of people, and the city beyond was alight with moving lanterns and torches. Behind them, to the east, the sun was rising, an orange glow building, as a pair of doves circled overhead.

"The reckoning has come for him."

Kira shook her head, hands trembling at her sides. She balled them into fists, fighting to remain outwardly calm. Alexandra grabbed her, dragging her to the head of the stairs. Faces turned to them—curiosity, suspicion, and anger. Kira swallowed, her gaze passing over them and fixing on the stream of torches making their way from the city gates far down the hill in the distance.

"What have you done?" Kira whispered.

"What has *he* done?" Alexandra bit back, a sneer in her voice.

"He's as he's always been." Kira's lips quivered, and she pressed them together to stop it. Tears threatened, a tightness constricting her throat. "He's the Saint."

"Hakan has overstepped. Started wars in the name of greed. Demanded power, and when it wasn't given, took it. He's misled us all. He's nothing but a man. A power-hungry, corrupt, flawed human being."

"No," Kira said, shaking her head. "You're lying."

"You're blind. You've been behind temple walls for too long, Oracle. Out there, the world has been changed by Hakan. But not for the better. When I brought you here, I thought things would be different. We had an oracle again after a generation without one. But he's bent you to his purpose, he's distorted your visions."

"No," Kira said, licking her lips, mind racing.

Where was Hakan? If they had him, Alexandra wouldn't be lecturing her in front of a crowd on the verge of rioting. She would be dealing with her fallen Saint, making sure she had the opportunity to slip a dagger between his ribs. The woman was speaking again, her voice low and full of menace.

"We don't want you," Alexandra said, glancing over the

younger woman, taking in the wound on the side of her face, the stained and ripped dress. "You were led astray. He took advantage of you. Do you realize that?"

Victim.

The word hung between them—unspoken. Kira didn't respond, staring out at the city in the predawn light. Torches moved along the streets, carried by men and women. A flowing river that met and merged, making its way to the temple perched above the city.

"He loves me."

"And how has that turned out for you?"

Kira swallowed, anger filling her chest, her hands balled into fists at her side.

"He's a god, Alexandra. The Saint. How do you think this will turn out for you?"

"He's nothing but a man." Alexandra smiled grimly. "And he'll die like one."

Kira took a step back toward the doors they'd come through, already considering where she might search for Hakan next. Alexandra's attention had moved on—dismissing Kira—as she went down to the waiting crowd.

"Find him if you can," Alexandra said over her shoulder. A hint of laughter lurked beneath her words. "Say your goodbyes. We start fresh with the dawn."

Kira fled as Alexandra went to meet the mob threading their way through the streets. A roiling mix of anger and shame filled her—to be dismissed like this, to be nothing worth fearing, to be nothing but an unimportant detail.

"And Kira," Alexandra said, the words stopping Kira in her tracks. "You are our oracle. You will always have a place with us, no matter what August says. Hakan's mistakes are not yours."

Chapter Five

Incense wafted through the halls—spicing the air with sandalwood and amber—clinging to Kira as she ran. Beneath it lay the stench of fear, the harsh copper slaughterhouse scents of blood and bile, and the oily smoke of torches. Her bare feet were silent as she ran from one circle of torchlight to the next. One hand kept her dress free of her legs while the other pressed to the wound on the side of her head.

These halls had been full of light and happiness, the temple grounds a maze of open spaces and shaded gardens. It was apart from the city, a sanctuary in a busy life, a place to retreat and reflect.

Kira had never truly believed in the Saint until she'd met him. Until she'd seen Hakan turn a fallow field to fruit or how he'd pulled back a soul from death. Those moments were few and far between, but they made a lasting impression.

Her gift, the ability to see and predict the future, had never seemed like anything out of the ordinary. Magic was alive in the world. It was as real as the earth beneath their feet or the sky overhead. But Hakan went beyond that—transcended it all. She'd loved her life within these walls. Kira loved the ability to use her gifts and the warmth she'd found so unexpectedly with Hakan.

Life would never be the same. Even if they survived this, so much had changed. The temple would never be a refuge; it would never be as welcoming as it had been. All faith in those around her had died.

And August? Could she trust August now?

Kira wasn't sure. Everything spun through her without stopping—this night, the banquet full of creatures, the sneer in Alexandra's voice, the heat of Hakan's kiss. Breath caught in her lungs and tears stinging her eyes, Kira ran, unable to think clearly.

Where was Hakan now?

The roof. He would be on the roof. Sometimes he went there to be alone. It overlooked the Citadel, perched almost at the peak, with only the palace above them. From there, the city marched down to the walls, plains visible for miles, and on a clear day, the mountains to the north.

Changing direction, Kira made her way to the stairs leading up. A door on the third floor opened onto the flat roof. If he wasn't there, then she had no idea where she might search next. And a part of her knew if he wasn't there, she would never see him again.

Please be there. Please.

When Kira reached the door, it was already open and waiting for her to walk through. She paused, catching her breath and trying to calm herself. If this was the end, she didn't want Hakan to see her cry. She needed to be strong. Not only for him, but for herself.

Noise washed over the building like a wave, reaching through the door and flowing over her. More people must have arrived—so many to make this constant susurration.

Kira pulled her shoulders back and went to see Hakan.

He stood looking over the city, arms crossed and shoulders

straight. Beyond him, the river of torches continued to flow uphill toward the temple.

"I didn't know where you were," Kira said, coming up behind him slowly. The accusation and frustration were clear in her voice.

Hakan turned to her, and she stopped, frozen by the expression of sorrow and pain on his face—tears filled his eyes but had not yet slipped free. When he held his arms open for her, she went to him, tucking herself against his side as they turned to face the city. They watched the people come, the sounds in the temple reaching a fever pitch. It was only a matter of time before they found him.

Tenderly, he pushed the hair away from her face, tilting her head slightly so he could get a better look at the seeping wound.

"Let me fix this," he murmured.

Hakan placed his palm against the spot, staring into her eyes as if they might kiss—as if they might embrace and forget this place.

There was no pop or sizzle, no tingling or slightest sensation. It was healed when he removed his hand, the blood now dry and flaking. The ache vanished, leaving her clearheaded.

"They're coming for you," she whispered, hating the words even as they left her mouth, hating the truth in them and what it would mean for their future—*her* future.

"I know," he said, squeezing her gently.

"I didn't see this!" Her voice rose as she spoke, his grip tightening.

"Not everything is visible to your inner eye, Oracle."

It was his temple voice, the solid tones that were law. That *had* been law. But no longer.

"I should have seen it," she whispered.

"Some things are hard to see," he said. "Even those who claim to be all-knowing never are."

"What will they do? The people down there." Kira asked, tilting her head back to search his face.

Hakan's expression was somber. What he would not say hung between them, heavy and full of sorrow. Kira squeezed her eyes shut, blocking the coming dawn but unable to stop the noise of the gathering crowd or halt the cold growing in her body.

"I should go down," he said. "They're gathering in the plaza now."

"We don't have to," she said, working to keep her voice calm. "We could leave. We could go anywhere."

"No, Kira." He shook his head, emotion flitting across his face so fast she was unable to read it. "This is where I must stay. They need me. But you don't have to remain. Go with August. There are other loyal temples. You could find a refuge out there."

"I won't leave you."

"What happens here will be hard," he said, placing his hands on her shoulders and staring down at her. "I don't want you to carry my death with you."

Kira shook her head. "Not knowing would be worse."

He nodded, mouth set in a grim line. The stones beneath her bare feet were cold. Soon, the sun would rise. Her feet would warm up. It would be a beautiful autumn day. Already, a handful of birds sang, and soft breezes carried the perfume of flowers and the scent of savory pastries from the bakers along Bakhous Row. Up here, away from the torches and the proximity of the crowd, it could have been any other day.

"Come," Hakan said, taking her hand. "We'll go together."

In silence, he led the way back down the stairs and through the temple complex, toward the plaza with its waiting mob. She concentrated on her breathing. In and out. Kira tried to silence the questions filling her mind—pulsing and hot.

Fear walked beside her with a somber step, a companion for this moment and all time. If Hakan felt it, he gave no indication. With his head held high, he looked as he always did—handsome, with chiseled features and elegant hands, his blue eyes shifting from light to dark. The blue she saw when he looked at her would always be her favorite color.

The temple appeared to be empty now, and they passed no one else. But she could feel the humanity waiting for them as they reached the main entrance. The doors were closed, but soon they would open onto the plaza, where the city met the temple grounds, going from mundane and hollow to sacred and profound.

Hakan turned to her, gathering her in his arms, fitting their bodies together until there was nothing between them but fabric. She longed to rip it off, to peel back the layers, and delay the moment he would release her. *Don't let me go.*

Wrapping her arms around his neck, she buried her face in his shoulder, breathing in deep—rich and slightly spicy with hints of deep blue water filling her senses. A sob caught in her throat, and she swallowed it, squeezing her eyes shut.

"Kira," Hakan whispered, rubbing his hands over her back—soothing her, comforting while he still could. "I love you in every lifetime. Do not ever doubt it."

She moved blindly, fumbling until she found his mouth. The kiss started softly, tender and tasting of tears, but he deepened it, their tongues meeting. She felt weightless in his arms, detached, except for where his hands gripped her and their mouths locked. Dark hunger churned through her—desperation, the need to have him overwhelming. It came from the desire to delay. To keep him with her. To remind them both that life was the most important thing.

But the future could not be held at bay.

Beyond the doors, a crowd hissed and seethed. A low vibration came up through the floor—hundreds of people, maybe thousands, were on the other side of the door. Soon, they would lose their patience and come searching.

Kira pulled away, studying his face, searching for their future in his eyes. He set her down gently and brushed her tears away, smoothing his thumb over her mouth. Cupping her face in his hands, Hakan pressed one more tender kiss to her lips.

"Do not try to stop what happens. Do not speak up. The most important thing you can do beyond those doors is to be anonymous," he murmured. "There are hard things ahead."

She nodded, reaching up to brush the tears on his cheeks, pulling him down until their foreheads touched. "I know."

"It's time," he said.

Kira nodded.

Hakan made a simple gesture with his left hand, and the massive doors swung outward—facing the dawn and the waiting crowd. Kira sucked in a breath. There were so many. More than she could count, more than she could guess at. When had so many people become angry? When had they turned on him? They were silent as the door opened, silent as Hakan squeezed her hand one more time before letting it go to step forward.

"The Saint is here." A single voice spoke.

Soon the phrase was repeated, growing and becoming a storm of noise. Hakan watched them, waiting for the words to die down, but they didn't. People were shouting for his death, others begging for his life.

At the foot of the stairs, Alexandra and Zavier stood—somber and silent.

Chapter Six

Without speaking, Hakan walked down the stairs toward the waiting group that stood apart from the others. The crowd pulled back, space growing around them until there was a large area cleared.

Kira slipped through the door and moved down the wide set of stairs, keeping her distance from Hakan and the others. Alexandra's gaze flicked to her and away. As the woman had said before, they weren't interested in Kira. At the foot of the stairs, Hakan stopped, waiting for them to speak.

"You have been judged and found wanting," Alexandra said, voice high and ringing out, silencing those who still spoke. "You've used the temple for your personal gain. It will no longer be tolerated."

"And what is your punishment?"

"Death."

A gasp rippled through the crowd.

Kira covered her mouth, pressing her hand hard against her lips to keep any noise from escaping. Cold and then hot pulsed through her, throbbing to the rhythm of the chanting crowd.

Death. Death. Death.

Kira searched the faces of the crowd—looking for the familiar, the every day—and saw August. She stood toward the back of the courtyard, eyes wide and mouth pressed into a thin line. While those around her shouted and raised their hands, she stood motionless. Briefly, their gazes met. August motioned for Kira to join her, but Kira shook her head, mouthing the words *not yet.*

Was there no one else? No one who would stand with him now? They'd abandoned the Saint to this fate. Their God. He'd taken too much over the last few years. Power. Wealth. Importance. He'd put the temple above the king and himself above them all.

She'd misjudged them—underestimated their anger, their number, and their determination. There had been whispers, her visions had been clouded, but she'd never truly worried about her place in the world. Even as she saw war and felt a distant growing fear, she'd been complacent.

Now they were paying the price.

They were paying for their arrogance.

The Saint spoke, his voice rolling out over the crowd, hands raised at his sides in a pacifying gesture. His voice was calmer than she could have managed. "This is not the way to do this."

"You are a false god!"

The words were angry, shouted from the middle of the crowd—faceless and defiant. A murmur of agreement rippled through the people, spreading and reaching her. A few around her glanced her way—furtive, curious.

"You've proven yourself to be nothing more than a man."

And what is so wrong with being that? Being human? she thought. As if it were such a crime to want to feel and be vulnerable. To have moments of weakness. But these people did not want a fallible being. They wanted perfection; they wanted a god above men, a creature who did not indulge in vices.

How could anyone—god or man—live up to such demands?

August had told her to run, that they would kill her if they found her. But Kira didn't think so, even now as she stood among them. They had seen her, and they'd looked away. There had been anger and disgust, resentment and even jealousy, but none had moved to hurt her.

They were saving everything for him.

"You cannot kill me," Hakan said, voice rising above the clamor.

"All men must die," Zavier said.

"This is a mistake," Hakan warned.

Alexandra scoffed, the corner of her mouth curling in a nasty smile. Hakan shook his head, resignation and sadness on his face, and it twisted Kira's heart to see the defeat there. Zavier laughed, the note sharp and cutting across the crowd, bringing all eyes to him.

"Do it," Alexandra said, making a cutting motion with her hand.

Her eyes shone with hatred, and Kira wondered why she'd never seen it before. Had it always been there? Or had Alexandra hidden her feelings? Or had Kira been too in love to pay attention when her mentor's attitude toward the Saint changed?

Zavier drew the sword at his side. Flames licked along the blade, almost invisible, but a sound crackled at the edge of hearing—a hissing rustle that made the hair on the back of Kira's neck stand up. Overhead, the sky darkened, the rising sun blotted out by gathering clouds rushing to fill the horizon. They moved in low to the ground, deep gray with rain and lightning.

As Zavier stalked forward, the flames on the sword flared

and his face twisted in pain. The crowd gasped as his sword hand blackened as if burned.

"Don't let go!" Alexandra urged as the man paused. "Push through the pain!"

Zavier nodded and reached Hakan, standing before him with terrible intention.

Without a word, Hakan knelt, hands at his side, face serene. His gaze didn't leave Zavier's face, locked on to the man, silently willing him to drop the sword or carry on. Kira had no way of knowing, but she refused to believe Hakan would accept death so easily.

The crowd hushed, whispers dying away as ominous silence overtook them. A bird called from one of the gardens farther in the temple, and thunder rumbled. Kira took a step forward, those around her pulling back, leaving her in a circle of space. She wanted to go to him, to stand between him and the priest. But he'd told her not to, and she had to listen to him, didn't she?

In one smooth motion, Zavier brought the burning sword up and thrust it into Hakan's chest. It slid in easily, past muscle and bone—up to the hilt—as Zavier twisted it with a cracking sound. A triumphant look filled the priest's face as he pulled the sword free.

"No!" Kira screamed as others cheered, their macabre joy turning her stomach.

Zavier dropped the sword, shaking his hand, and the blood drained from his face. His sword arm blackened, the sickening scent of cooking flesh filling the air. The burning sword hit the paving stones and melted through, sinking into the hard surface. A ribbon of flames rose, sparking and dancing, reaching several feet into the air. The blade continued to sink. The earth eased open, swallowing it in one swift gulp. In the silence, only a singed patch of stone remained.

Kira pushed forward, falling to her knees before Hakan,

hitting the stones hard—bruising tender flesh—and reaching for him. Her fingers shook, anguish and disbelief expanding in her chest. They always knelt for each other—treating each other as equals in their secret moments. Now she let them all —those in her order and the people from beyond the temple doors—see her love and devotion.

But Hakan wasn't aware of her. His face paled as the blood left him—eyes distant, expression serene. No pain or fear, nothing but the quietness of his life draining away.

She eased him down, his head in her lap, and his face turned up to the morning sky. The blood on his chest was crusted—not wet or drying—but something else. The substance glittered. With trembling fingers, she touched the fabric, the ruby crystals hard beneath her hand. She tried to move them, searching for a wound to place her hand against. But there was no opening.

"Hakan," she whispered, brushing the hair from his face, mind racing. "What's happening to you?"

If he heard her, if he knew it was her lap he rested in, he gave no sign. A shudder passed through him. Then his eyes rolled back, nothing but whites visible, as he began to thrash. A flailing arm caught her across the face, and she scrambled back with a cry of pain. Hakan's head hit the stone with a sharp crack. The worn marble beneath him shattered, cracks zigzagging out from his body, spreading across the courtyard in seconds.

His tan skin shivered, crawling as if something other than muscle moved beneath the surface. Blood pooled and seeped from his eyes and nose—running down his cheeks and over his lips, teeth bared and gory.

Kira covered her mouth, fighting to keep in a scream. The liquid crystalized—forming jewels, cut and polished precious stones. Blood red rubies. His flesh melted, shrinking, disappearing millimeter by millimeter, as the bones beneath expanded. Hakan grew, his skeleton shining wetly—golden like the rays of the rising sun, red like rubies held up to a fire.

The crowd gasped, murmurs turning into cries of surprise and fear. Several people took a step back, hands pressed flat to their chests to keep their panicking hearts in place. Kira's own raced—a frantic rhythm fighting to keep up, to keep going, even as dread caught her by the throat and squeezed.

"The Saint lives!" a man shouted.

With those words, the watchers turned and ran.

Kira remained. Unable to look away.

What lay in the courtyard belonged to a creature ten feet tall. Each bone was gilded, organs becoming precious stones—rubies and emeralds—cut and polished as if a meticulous jeweler had put together this beautiful and monstrous creation. Legs joined hips, spine and ribcage, arms and hands, and the stretched, grinning skull that had been the beautiful face of her lover. The pieces joined and held as if by magic.

It must be, she realized. Because how else could he stay together? His bones were kept in place by gods' blood—immortality. *Hakan*.

The creature sat up, turning slowly, surveying the remaining believers, and stopping when it saw Zavier. The man groaned, the noise coming from low in the gut—wrenching and filled with dreadful knowledge. He'd frozen in place. The surrounding people covered their mouths or faces or ears. They knew without needing to be told, but a collective fear kept them in place.

The Saint—the god—stretched out a long arm, impossibly alive, and snatched the priest by his burned arm, dragging him forward. Zavier went quietly, stunned into silence. But others screamed. They screamed *for* him—horrified.

As the Saint opened his mouth and leaned down to bite, Kira turned away, unable to watch. Zavier's anguish filled her head, and bile crawled up her throat. *Don't. Please stop.*

Hakan. But she stood motionless, eyes wide and staring straight ahead as tears rolled down her cheeks. The Saint took another bite. Another. Horrible sounds of flesh and bone breaking—ripping. Something hit the marble with a wet smack.

Members of her order ran, slipping past those in the crowd who watched transfixed. Some knelt, weeping and tearing at their robes. Others were silent. A few feet away, a man had fainted. A woman beside him patted his face desperately, whispering something Kira couldn't understand. Zavier was gone. Mastication finished. But Kira could not bring herself to face what had become of the man she loved.

A skittering, scraping sound reached her as the Saint stood. Kira watched as those around her tilted their heads back, following his rise like sunflowers following the sun.

"He lives."

The words were picked up and carried on—whispers of awe, low tones filled with terror. *He lives.*

But he was no longer a man. *No*, she corrected herself, *he no longer wore the skin of a man.* Kira turned, unable to delay the moment any longer, needing to see the reality of this change for herself.

A skeleton towered over the crowd—a beautiful being, glimmering and gilded, a living relic in the fresh dawn. A pale translucent shimmer overlaid his body, and in the deep sockets of his skull, a pale light burned. He was easily ten feet tall, well beyond the over six feet he'd been in life. He'd grown in his brutal transformation, becoming this precious monster.

The Saint's inhuman gaze found her, the golden light flaring with recognition.

Her lover. Her god.

The Saint thrust a hand into his chest. Golden ribs shifted, groaning with pressure as he grasped his glittering ruby heart. He wrenched it free—a handful of cut rubies, a mass of stones that mimicked one of flesh and blood—as an eerie quiet throbbed through the crowd. The Saint took a step toward her, his hand out. A few faces turned to her, pale ovals, sunlight catching on eyelashes, long shadows racing across the courtyard. Somewhere, a sparrow sang.

Kira covered her mouth as the Saint reached her, holding his heart—a sacrifice or gift.

The only thing she'd ever truly wanted.

He knelt and offered the precious object. With trembling fingers, she took his heart, and the warmth of it filled her, the hard, polished surface slick in her sweaty hands. She studied it; her face reflected in the surface, highlighting the fire twisting at the center.

A sob broke from her chest, wordless and carrying an ocean of grief and loss. The Saint extended a hand, palm up. A tentative question. But Kira stepped back with a small shake of her head. *No.* Her throat closed around the word, but he knew by her reaction. He looked down at his hands—golden bones covered in blood, his teeth slick with it. With a small inclination of his head, he stood.

The Saint turned, striking like a snake, grabbing another red-robed priest. The man screamed, the pitch climbing as teeth sank into flesh. Tearing and rending followed, pieces splattering down.

Kira shut her eyes, bile rising in her throat. The remaining crowd scattered, bumping and jostling her. Somewhere in the city, a bell rang out in warning.

Kira clutched the last gift from her lover, waiting for the world to stop—for it to end here with him. But it continued, time spinning out and expanding in circles with the Saint at the center. Reaching the courtyard gates, poised between the temple and city, he paused. The rising sun caught him, haloing him in light—a beautiful monster. Someone screamed. The long wail spiraled up as a horn from the castle battlements broke through.

The Saint went out into the city.

"Death is not the end," she whispered, clutching the glittering remains of Hakan's heart. "This is not *our* end."

What Came After

Five years of terror followed.

The Saint called the monsters of the world to him, creatures from nightmares and the edges of dreams coming out of the shadows to help him take and maintain power. Old magic overtook the continent and held sway. His believers grew in number, the ranks swelling as temples were built overnight. Kira stood at his side in his court, dressed in gold and wearing rubies—the revered oracle and confidant of the Saint. Sacrifices were demanded and made. Anyone who refused was killed.

But the broken kingdoms united, drawn together in their desperation. Those who had risen against the Saint once before rose again. He was torn apart and scattered—relics placed in protected temples or hidden until it was safe to bring them out once more. Kira led those who remained faithful, a new religion growing out of the old, turning the horror of the past into a story of salvation and peace.

Four hundred years have passed since the transformation of the Saint. His acolytes believe he will be resurrected. He will return to lead them and bring peace to their war-torn lives.

But the truth of the past has been almost forgotten, romanticized in stories, and only his ability to return from death is remembered.

But what do dead gods know of the living?

What returns when you wake the dead?

The Dead Saint - Book One
The Living Saint - Book Two
Steel and Starlight - Companion Novella

KEEP READING FOR A SNEAK
PEEK AT THE DEAD SAINT

The Dead Saint - Chapter One

The city screamed as fire ate it alive.

Overhead, a gray sky swirled, large flakes of snow liquefying and then evaporating before the moisture could reach the burning buildings. Flames crackled and danced, sending joyous greedy tendrils over stone and wood—hungry and murmuring, expanding as it ate. Places once so familiar—the villas and temples Sorcha saw every day—were in ruins.

A thousand tiny fires—cracking and insatiable—converged to consume and transform, revealing the bones of a fallen civilization. Ash drifted around Sorcha, dancing on updrafts and settling between cobblestones and on window ledges, a flurrying storm of destruction and despair. The high castle at the center of Golden Citadel was a column of fierce fire, the huge stones at the base buckling under the weight of the sagging upper towers.

As she watched, the gold on the minarets was melting, rivers of molten metal coursing over the stones. She couldn't see it from here, but she knew it would be running down the streets, flowing downhill. Eventually, if enough of it melted, it would reach the outer walls.

There were no other noises beyond the fire. No one screamed or spoke, no one cried or whispered. There was no one left to do those things. They were all dead.

The gates had shattered, then the walls had been breached, and once inside, the horde had killed anyone who survived the siege. There hadn't been so many of them left. Not at the end. Half the city had gone to the White Snake—the child of an assassinated emperor, son of a revered empress—a ruling prince and merciless tyrant. He'd offered favorable terms: come willingly, be under my rule, and live.

Living was all that mattered.

The rest had been slaughtered.

Sorcha hurried down the center of Ruby Road. There were no shadows to hide in, no place to find cover. The only way to avoid the fire was to walk down the middle of the main road that spiraled from the Citadel gates to the high castle. The other roads were narrow, villas only a few feet apart in places, with footbridges built to connect buildings, potted plants and vines trained over wooden arches. People lived as much in the streets of the Golden Citadel as their homes here.

Had. She corrected herself. *Had lived.*

The stink of singed hair clung to her, the strands of golden thread and pearls hopelessly tangled in her messy dark braids. Her left shoulder throbbed painfully, relentlessly, as a result of a falling ornament in the temple. The gown clung to her, wet with the blood of the final ritual, the bodies of those she'd come across in the streets, and one bloody knee. She'd tripped and landed hard in the courtyard before the temple gates. Each breath pulled in fine drifting ash, leaving her eyes and lips gritty and the back of her throat coated.

Sorcha wanted a cool drink of water and shade, the comfort of a plush sofa with downy feather cushions and fresh silk against her skin. Already, her last meal haunted her—the uneaten chicken, a pear with only a single bite taken from it, and a goblet of wine left half-full. There was nothing like that behind her anymore and nothing like it ahead.

Run, Rohan had said. *Make your way out of the city. Find the Androphagoi dedicated to the Saint. Always go south, keep the golden star burning on the horizon to your right—keep to it faithfully—it is a symbol, a sign that the Saint will return soon.*

Then everyone, even the White Snake, would know the true power of the god.

The star would lead her to safety. It meant hope. Beneath it, she would find someone who could help her. Someone to guide her. Sorcha was going to need their help to find all the scattered relics, to do what she'd been born to do, and resurrect the Saint.

But it would take time.

Time was an enemy as great as the horde.

Both waited for Sorcha beyond the city gates.

A soldier found her before she reached the fourth switchback in Ruby Road.

The street had been empty, and the growl of the fire rumbled around her, beams crashing in a shower of sparks and splinters, roofs collapsing in waves. A street away, a temple to a minor god shivered and came crashing down, stones exploding outward, crashing into the surrounding buildings and sending out a dark cloud that reached her.

A distraction, only a second of distraction, and in that moment, a man appeared a few feet in front of her. She stopped, hand going to her mouth in surprise, smothering the exclamation of fear. She froze, cursing herself for hesitating, cursing the fear that coursed through her veins while her legs refused to move.

He smiled, pale eyes glittering with hunger, rough features

with hair shaved close to his skull, and a fresh scar running from temple to ear. When he spoke, the words were harsh, coming from deep in his chest, but she couldn't understand the language.

Shaking her head, she took a step back, mouth dry and unable to speak. Another step, and for a brief moment, she wondered if she might be able to outrun him.

But he moved swiftly, darting forward and blocking her path, closing the distance between them in a blink. He leaned in, his face inches from her own. Foul breath washed over her face, metallic and sharp, and with a shudder, she realized his mouth was dark with a mix of blood and ash.

"Don't touch me," she whispered, clearing her throat and repeating the words with more strength.

The man laughed, throwing back his head, eyes squinting and half-shut.

Sorcha leaned away, looking around wildly for someone, anyone. *There is no one left. They're all dead.* She stepped closer, kicking his shin, her soft slipper coming up against thick, studded leather.

His laugh deepened, the bite of his fingers becoming unbearable.

"Help!" she screamed, frustrated with herself for wasting precious energy. There would be no help for her now.

"Help!" The man mimicked her—mocking her—the word strange in his mouth. He spoke again, accent distorting his language, but she caught it clearly enough. "There is no one to save you."

And of course, he was right. She knew it.

But a flicker of movement over his shoulder stopped her heart. Someone else was alive.

A tall, ashen man walked calmly up behind her captor, eyes an unusual pale yellow, flat and dead looking. His face was expressionless in the flicker of firelight. Without speaking, he thrust a dagger into her captor's back, holding Sorcha's horrified gaze, twisting the blade with a jerk of the wrist.

Sorcha stumbled back, the dying man going with her, his weight taking her to the ground. They landed together in a heap, pain shooting through her as she was caught between the weight of the man and the cobblestones.

Her captor tried to roll, eyes wide, mouth open, his grip on her finally easing.

But the stranger followed him down, plunging the blade into his back again and again, the motion frenzied even as his face stayed emotionless.

Sorcha sat frozen, unable to move, a scream echoing through her mind even as her voice failed her.

Get up! Run!

As if the man had heard her internal voice, he turned to her, eyes flat, mouth set in a thin line. Blood freckled his cheeks, larger drops on his black armor, and it dripped from the hand still gripping the blade. The attacker wiped the blade on the dead man's cloak, eyes leaving her face for a second.

She surged to her feet and bolted, gathering up the crimson dress, desperate to avoid tripping over it. But the man was up and moving more quickly than she'd anticipated, following with a creak of leather and rattle of chainmail.

Sorcha glanced around, mind racing. The buildings to either side were burning. There was nowhere to run. She made the decision in an instant, cutting to the left, focused on an open doorway where fire burned beyond.

The man grabbed her, jerking her backward, away from the flames she'd been so eager to embrace.

"Don't be a fool," he hissed, blackened teeth flashing. "There is someone who wants to meet you."

His accent was strange, but he spoke her language more smoothly than the last man had. Even if she hadn't, his message was clear. *Don't die before I get a chance to kill you.* She didn't bother to answer, fighting his grip, twisting and hoping to dislodge his strong fingers.

He watched her, a hunter studying a rabbit caught in a snare—dispassionate and calculating.

The look made her skin crawl.

This man was more dangerous than the other one had been.

Without another word, he began walking, dragging her behind him, keeping a tight hold on her wrist. He didn't pause when she stumbled, keeping her upright through force and determination.

She gasped as her bones creaked, squeezed together, and wondered if he'd break her wrist before they reached whatever destination he had in mind.

Sorcha's head felt fuzzy, disconnected from the world around her as she stumbled down Ruby Road beside this stranger. Her mind spun back, returning to the temple of the Saint and her final moments there. She tried to see what was around her, ground herself to this moment, but it was just as horrible as what had already happened. The memory, the horror of it, came to her like the visions that had been a constant since her childhood.

Blood. There had been so much blood. Spreading out, reflecting the fires, reminding her she had promises to keep. The faces of her friends and family, the temple elders and youngsters, the people she loved.

Tears threatened, a stone in her throat, lungs gasping on the verge of giving way to heaving sobs.

No. She wouldn't expose those parts of herself, her terror and sorrow, the weight that had settled so completely in her bones. *Don't think about it.* She would escape this man and find her way out of the city still. There was a chance, she was still alive, and there was always hope.

Turning her attention to the part of the city they were

now moving through, she was surprised to see how far they'd come. They were close to the outer wall here. It towered above her, throwing deep shadows across thatched and tiled rooftops, the shade beginning to scatter and flee as the fire spread out from the city center.

The man steered her down another street, a smaller one branching off Ruby Road, one that led toward one of the larger plazas near the main gate. They passed shopfronts with shattered windows, glass glimmering on the ground—reflecting firelight—splashes of blood on the walls and cobblestones. But no bodies that she could see.

In a way, that was worse. To know people had died, to see the evidence, but not the bodies. Where had they been taken? Or had they risen from death to walk the streets like the old legends?

A shiver rippled through Sorcha, cold lingering as they rounded another corner and came out into a plaza with a fountain bubbling at the center.

The area was full of armor-clad figures with their hands on their weapons.

All eyes focused on her.

Sorcha lifted her chin. Countless times, she'd moved through King Roi court, talking with advisors or generals, courtesans, or minor nobility. She knew who she was in every room she entered. There had been men as bloodthirsty as any in the Empire of the White Snake. She'd passed among them all—oracle and extension of the Saint—without ever questioning her safety. But this was different. These were the men who had brought the Golden Citadel to its knees.

"Keep walking."

Her captor moved Sorcha forward when she hesitated. If the man who gripped her arm so tightly wasn't in charge, who would be?

Then she saw him. Sorcha stopped, brows pulling together, curious despite herself.

The man radiated power, an intensity that pulled the eye and forced everyone else into the background. He had unusual features, with hair and eyes as black as onyx, which made her think of silence at midnight. No stars, no moon, only a watchful void. The black armor and leather gloves he wore were as dark, the war horse beneath him a similar shade. A white wolf skull was tied to the saddle. They said he wore it into battle, that his sword was always wet, that the blood on his hands would never dry.

The Kingdom Killer. The monster. The Wolf.

The Dead Saint - Chapter Two

Adrian had been instructed to find the Saint's vessel—a young woman, twenty-two years old, with dark hair and blue-green eyes. The description had come from a high-ranking temple priestess who had come to the prince. The woman had said the vessel would have tattoos—a history and map of the dead Saint on her skin. She might try to hide her identity, but those, she wouldn't be able to hide.

Her skin told his story, her flesh would point the way.

So far, they hadn't located the woman. But it was only a matter of time.

All hope for a reprieve from the death sentence that was the empire's ever-conquering horde had died as the gates fell inward and the fires took hold. If there was anyone else left alive in the city, they would know her, and they might give her away when the pain became unbearable and release was offered. If there was no one to give her up, he would search each building, even as they burned and fell around him.

He refused to accept that she might have perished in the fire.

Prince Eine had offered riches beyond measure in

exchange for the woman: promotion to Adrian's personal unit —the Tomeis—enough gold to last several lifetimes and a personal favor from the prince himself. The favor, the ear of the prince, was the most prized. It would be something to hold tight in the face of the long months ahead and coming battles.

Anyone would welcome these rewards. Each man listening had been hungry, ready for the pale light of morning as the siege came to an end, so they would have the chance to enter the city and find the woman.

"What do we do when we find her?"

A man had asked, a stranger unknown to Adrian. The others in the crowd had turned to him, focusing hard eyes on Adrian, searching for any hint of deception.

"Bring her to me."

The men had nodded, more than a hundred of them fanning out into the city as the gates came down. His own men, the Black Teeth led by Revenant, were already gone, moving on Adrian's private orders.

Find the woman as quickly and quietly as possible.

Make sure no one else did.

Adrian saw the woman before she saw him. Revenant marched her toward the group of waiting men, his face blank but eyes blazing, as the woman fought him. She pried at his fingers, working to loosen his grip, but she grimaced when he squeezed. She was singed and dirty, the hem of her crimson dress dark with blood and the long, loose sleeves torn. Her hair was a wild black halo around her pale face, bits of gold and jewels tangled in the mess.

This was the woman the prince wanted?

Adrian considered her, cataloging details, collecting what he might be able to use to his advantage later. She didn't look like a woman of wealth and power. Or whatever it was she was supposed to be. She was bejeweled and wearing fine things, however damaged, but without an air of command. He would have passed over her in a crowd without a second glance, a forgettable woman in a sea of faces and nothing like what he'd pictured.

An oracle, priestess, and vessel of the Saint.

Her gaze landed on him finally—the only man on a horse in the square—and the shock of her anger sizzled between them. Her eyes narrowed and her mouth opened as if she planned to yell for help or yell at him. He couldn't be sure. But the directness of her expression and the fury in it changed everything. It transformed her face. The woman's eyes were a vibrant, striking green. His breath caught, stuck in his lungs as an arrow of desire pierced him, lodging in his chest—a dangerous surprise.

But the anger in her gaze shifted, eyes widening, skin going pale as she realized who she was being taken to. Understanding settled in her features, her knuckles white with pressure as she squeezed her hands into fists.

Monster.

She didn't need to speak the word for him to hear it. It filled the air around them all. He saw it on her face, the moment of realization. A tall man on a black horse—black armor, black gloves, wearing the bone-white skull of a monstrous wolf.

The Wolf. The City Slayer. The Kingdom Killer.

The monster who wanted her.

Revenant jerked her to a halt several feet away, out of reach from his horse's sharp bite. Nox shifted beneath him, skin twitching, turning to look at the pair who'd dared to come so close.

Adrian didn't speak—waiting, watching the woman. She hadn't looked at him again, her eyes elsewhere, searching for an easy place to rest. But there wasn't one. Everywhere she looked, there was fire and death.

"Here is the woman—" Revenant tugged at her sleeve, pulling it back to reveal a tattoo. Black ink crawled up her arm and disappeared beneath the fabric.

She tried to pull free, twisting in Revenant's grasp, but the man tightened his grip until she cried out and her knees buckled.

"Enough," Adrian said.

His voice was soft, but every single man in the square turned their attention to the three standing together. He could feel their curiosity, even bitterness at not being the one who found the woman. Revenant didn't want or need favors from Prince Eine. Those gifts were wasted on such a creature.

Revenant's brows lifted slightly with Adrian's orders. It was more emotion than the man generally showed, but he quickly smoothed his expression, easing the pressure on the woman's wrist.

"Are you the vessel?" Adrian asked, studying her.

She shook her head, glancing at him and away, searching for an escape. She was tense, poised to run, stubbornness plain in her features and the way she held herself. A flicker of humor shot through him. She was afraid, that was clear, but that she held on to her anger.

"Do you know who I am?"

She nodded once.

Adrian raised an eyebrow, waiting to see if she would say more. When she didn't, he looked to Revenant. "Was anyone else with her?"

"Lane had her. I killed him."

Adrian swore internally. Lane had crossed Revenant a month ago, leaving the man in a difficult position during a battle. Revenant had promised to repay him for that favor, and he'd finally had the opportunity. But that was something

Adrian would address when there was no one else to overhear.

"Give her to me," he said.

Revenant shoved the woman toward the horse. Nox snorted and stamped in warning at the sudden movement.

She caught her balance and flashed Revenant a glare. Her gaze came back to Adrian before shifting away, still searching for a way out.

Adrian held out a gloved hand, palm tingling, wondering if she'd bolt or stand her ground. He waited for her to accept his offer, but she silently refused. Nox sidestepped beneath him, uneasy with his rider's sudden tension.

"You ride with me or them," Adrian said.

The woman glanced at the watching men and then over her shoulder to where Revenant stood with that dead flat expression he'd perfected. He bared his blackened teeth in a snarl, and the woman paled.

"You're an animal to them. They will not hesitate to kill you."

It was a lie. Anyone who touched this woman would die. But she didn't need to know it.

"And you won't?" she asked, meeting his gaze with a challenge.

Revenant stepped forward and shoved her, sending the woman stumbling into Adrian's grasp. Before she could twist away or cry out, he had a hold of her, pulling her up into the saddle. He shifted, his arms a cage around her, as she settled on his lap. The scent of smoke and singed hair came with her, and below that, the copper stink of blood and fear. She sat ridged in an effort not to touch him, breathing heavily.

"Make sure there are no survivors," Adrian said with a nod to Revenant and the others.

They brought their right fist to their hearts in acknowledgment and a salute as he turned Nox toward the main gate. The woman shifted, leaning forward as much as possible, slipping as the horse walked.

"Do you want to fall and be trampled?"

When she didn't respond, he looped an arm around her waist, pulling her into his body. Even with clothes and armor between them, he felt her soft warmth, and it sent a shiver racing over him. Her hair brushed his face, the top of her head bumping his chin, as he urged Nox across the square. Adrian worked to ignore the feel of her against him, the way she trembled, her hands balled into fists.

He tiled his head to get a better look at her, catching a curve of her cheek and the sweep of thick lashes.

"I won't hurt you," he said.

She half turned to him—green eyes wary—her distaste a physical force. "I'm not stupid enough to trust a monster."

There, she'd said it aloud. Her tone was as sharp as his had been soft—words cutting like broken glass flung at him with full force. It could not have sat so long between them without being given solid form.

He smiled grimly, a part of him pleased that he'd pulled a reaction from her—pleased with her anger.

An angry woman was easier to deal with than a sad one. He had no time for tears. But anger he understood. Anger he could handle. Sorrow, tears, the wailing of deep wounds was something he had wanted to avoid at all costs.

The woman in his arms would never give him her tears; he'd known it the moment their eyes met. Adrian could feel her making promises to herself, the frantic whirling of her mind and emotions. She would give him as little of herself as possible. But he would take everything from her.

Just as he's taken this city. Already, the fires had eaten so much of it. The death cries of the survivors had been silenced hours ago. There was no more clashing metal, no more shouts or pleas. There was no one left.

Those who had taken the prince's offer had left weeks ago, already moved on to live beneath the eaves of the Traveling City or sent to the farthest edges of the empire. Those who had held out, remaining in the city because they thought the prince's soft-spoken voice made him weak, were all dead.

Prince Eine might be soft spoken, but the edge of his blade was sharp and his mind cruel. There would have been torture and mutilation before death, incredible pain and despair. Repayment for the insult their refusal had caused. But soothing his own emotions wasn't the prince's only goal. The stories of what happened spread and were another weapon against those who challenged his dreams of expanding the empire.

The woman jerked in his arms and gasped. There were bodies in the streets here near the main gate. Blood pooled between cobblestones and on the flat pavers. The stink of gore fought to overpower the smoke, a foul scent that would cling to his clothes and stick in his nostrils for the next several days.

"You did this." Her voice was a harsh whisper, emotion choking her. "You killed them all."

He remained silent, unable to and uninterested in denying it.

"You truly are a monster," she hissed, twisting abruptly in his arms, wriggling until his hold slipped and she dropped to the cobbles.

The horse lunged for her, teeth snapping, and Adrian twitched the bridle in a warning. Nox quieted, ears laid back.

The woman scrambled away, panting and pushing awkwardly to her feet. She turned in a circle, taking in her surroundings and freezing as she looked out over the main road leading away from the Golden Citadel.

preorder The Dead Saint and continue the adventure...

About the Author

Kathryn Trattner is an award-winning author who has loved fairy tales, folk stories, and mythology all her life. Her hands-down favorites have always been East of the Sun, West of the Moon and the myth of Persephone and Hades. When not writing or reading, she's traveling as much as possible and taking thousands of photos that probably won't get edited later. She lives in Oklahoma with her wonderful husband, two very busy children, one of the friendliest dogs ever, and three cats who think they're in charge.

If you enjoyed this book, please consider leaving a review and signing up for my newsletter. You'll get information on new releases and exclusive content!

https://www.kathryntrattner.com/newsletter

- facebook.com/kathryntrattner
- instagram.com/k.trattner.author
- bookbub.com/authors/kathryn-trattner
- tiktok.com/@kathryntrattnerauthor
- goodreads.com/kathryntrattner

Also by Kathryn Trattner

Deep Water and Other Stories

Mistress of Death

The Scent of Leaves

Magic and Myth: Short Stories

Magnolia House

The Glass Palace

<u>The Blood and Rubies Series</u>

Sacrament and Smoke

The Dead Saint

The Living Saint

Steel and Starlight

<u>Coming Soon</u>

The Sparrow King and Other Stories

Made in the USA
Columbia, SC
09 March 2025